CW01508090

This is entirely a work of fiction, pulled out of my own imagination. All characters and events are not real (fictitious). If there are any similarities to real persons, living or dead, it is purely coincidental.

I have never had my home invaded, nor have I ever invaded anyone's home.

I do not know anyone who has ever invaded a home.

These characters are fiction (fake). Not based upon true events.

Hopefully, you will find this very realistic, even if it's entirely false.

On the cover, that very well may be a very filtered and squished photo of my own home.

MAYBE

Description

A noise wakes a sleeping husband and wife.
Two intruders.
With a gun to their heads, the married couple has to complete a series of tasks by hurting each other.
A sadistic game designed to test the idea of 'love' and 'being in love'.
Would you rather physically torture the one you love? Or would you rather allow your lover to physically torture you?

WARNING: This book involves multiple scenes of torture. This is an extremely violent book.

Part One: Meet the Fam

Sneak

The Boston terrier at his feet was making the already hard task of sneaking into the quiet home a nearly impossible task. "I've only been gone a few hours. You act like you haven't seen me in a year," Dylan whispered as he tried to bend down and pat the pup. The combination of being low to the ground, and the dog's stumped-tail rapidly moving side-to-side like windshield wipers in a hard rain, caused him to stumble.

Denial. Anything other than those two extra beers he had. In his mind, Dylan did not want to admit that he had drank too much, once again.

The family pet accepted a treat and made his way back upstairs to Angelica's room, where his small bed awaited for him. The pooch loved all their family members, but especially their daughter. Perhaps because she played with him more than anyone else.

If anyone else had been awake, they would have heard the canine's toenails sliding across the hardwood floor, scampering away with its treasure in its mouth.

Dylan had more important matters to attend to. An aching bladder.

As he flushed the toilet of the en suite bathroom, Dylan flinched, in fear that he would wake his sleeping wife. Drinking too many beers on his boys' night had lapsed his judgment, despite his denial, and now he was cursing himself for not using the hallway bathroom.

Past experience had taught him that on occasion the swirling water sounds would wake Stella. Lately she had been working overtime at her job as a pharmacist, but finally she had gotten a weekend off from work. If anyone needed a good night of rest, Dylan knew it would be his wife that deserved it.

He was thankful as he fumbled his way to their bed that she was unmoving, other than the rise and fall of her chest that corresponded with her small snores. The fact that he got home more than an hour later than he promised he would be home was enough to send chills up his spine.

The clock read a little past one in the morning. In his head, Dylan rehearsed his lie in case Stella did ask why he was home so late. *Honey, I'm sorry, but the game ran a tad late, then we had to celebrate the win.*

Making the wife angry was never a good thing. If her mood was sour the next day, it would make his hangover double worse. An aching head was never a good thing, especially if Stella was harping on him on his day off from work.

Dylan removed his clothes, using the wall for support to ensure that he wouldn't fall to the ground while sliding his pants off his legs. When he left the club, he hadn't felt as drunk as he was now, and it made him wonder how he drove home.

A chuckle escaped his lips after he imagined what it would have been like to phone his sleeping wife if he had been arrested for drunk driving. Once again, he had been lucky. As far as his memory serves, he didn't wreck their shared vehicle, and him standing in the bedroom was proof that he didn't go to jail.

His faint laughter must have been louder than he thought because Stella did move, shifting from her back to her side, placing her backside towards her husband's side of the bed.

Fate was working in his favor. With her back to him, she wouldn't be able to smell the beer on his breath, or the scent of another woman. Not that he could smell other women on him. Dylan thought it was a mystery as to why strippers would practically bathe themselves in perfume, knowing that married men would have to explain that when they got home.

Those kinds of girls, he always avoided if he could.

If the most attractive girl in the club wore too much fragrance, Dylan didn't mind lowering his standards and settling for a less attractive, non-smelling female.

Naturally, Stella didn't know he had been at a strip club. His alibi was a sports game, one that he checked the scores on his phone before arriving home, just in case she were awake and asked. The game had been broadcast on the wall at the club, but the stage performers were far more interesting to watch.

Stella thought it was a typical night out with guys, at a sports bar. Buckets of beer. Chicken wings. Sports. The only other women, in her imagination, were waitresses and other customers.

Dylan did love his wife. She was the best mother he could imagine for their two children and would never intentionally hurt her feelings. But after twenty years of marriage, she had packed on a few pounds, which really didn't bother him. It did bother her, though, by his math, because their intimacy had declined in the past few years.

His own logic was that she was either insecure of herself, which she shouldn't be because he made every effort to let her know that he still desired her sexually. Either that, or maybe she wasn't attracted to him any longer. His own belly wasn't as flat as when they first wed.

If, by chance, he got lucky at the club and one of the naked women were willing to pleasure him, Dylan wasn't one to say no. Sex didn't change any of his feelings towards his wife. It was nothing more than a physical act. Zero emotions involved. And it wasn't like the women lined up to be with him, unless he had a pocket of spare cash.

His rationalization was that if he didn't carry on an ongoing relationship with another woman, then he had fulfilled his side of their wedding vows.

Carefully, he slid into the bed, him also turning his back to her, trying his best not to touch Stella.

The sound of her snoring pleased him, and he closed his eyes, feeling safe and content that she would never know what time he got home.

His only hope was that his luck would continue into the next morning and she wouldn't have a to-do list a mile long of household chores. It would be much easier to nurse his hangover by sitting on the couch, watching television, and neglecting the yard work.

HungedOver

"Daddy! Daddy!" Angelica exclaimed as she jumped on her father's bed, causing it to bounce his entire body. "Mommy made pancakes. With blueberries! Your favorite!"

His eyes didn't want to open, and the bed bouncing did him no favors as far as his aching head and queasy stomach were concerned. Dylan groaned, but tried his best to smile anyway.

"Honey, Daddy had a late night, and he worked hard all week." Stella's voice carried down the hallway from the kitchen. "Angelica, I'll save him some leftovers."

Without warning, Dylan lunged up, both hands gripped around his six-year-old daughter's belly. "The tickle monster is awake!"

"Mommy! Daddy is tickling me!"

It hurt every muscle in Dylan's aging body, but hearing Angelica's laughter and smelling the blueberry pancakes was enough to motivate him out of bed. "Honey, go tell Mommy that I'll be in there in a minute. Is Brandon awake?"

"Yeah, but all he wants to do is play his video game. He's upstairs."

A small growl from the floor let Dylan know that their Boston terrier was waiting patiently on the floor. "Why don't you take Tux in the kitchen? I'll be in there soon, I promise." It wouldn't be unusual if his daughter saw him in his boxer shorts, but Dylan tried to avoid it whenever he could.

Tux, short for Tuxedo, was appropriate for the smallish dog. The way his black fur covered his back, but opened down his chest into white fur, made it appear the dog was wearing a suit jacket and dress shirt. Right down to a rise in the white fur around Tux's neck, resembling a collar.

In times like now, he was thankful for the attached bathroom. Pants could wait until after he relieved himself. The room was spinning, but only slightly, and the ache behind his eye wasn't the worst throb he had ever experienced.

Pajama bottoms were easy enough with the elastic waist, paired with a plain white T-shirt, and Dylan was good to go.

A fake grin quickly turned into a genuine smile as Dylan stood at the entrance of the kitchen, admiring his wife in her silk pajamas and apron, her face covered in splotches of pancake mix.

"Mom, how long until we eat?" Brandon asked as he entered the room from the other hallway. The wireless headphones were hanging loosely around his ears. It wasn't unusual for the eight-year-boy to pause a gaming session if it were hunger related. "I have a few friends waiting for me."

"Friends?" Dylan questioned. "Waiting for you? Where are they? In the front yard or something?"

"No, Dad. They're online. You know that. They live far away. Maybe I'll get a chance to meet them in real life one day."

"Yeah, maybe." Stepping up behind his wife, Dylan leaned in close and kissed the back of her head and observed that the largest pancake was shaped as a heart. "That must be mine. It smells great, honey."

"Good morning," Stella replied, briefly turning her head and allowing her husband the opportunity to kiss her cheek. "I told Angelica not to wake you. I figured you were tired after last night. I saw the Cats won and figured you may have celebrated later than your usual."

"You know me too well. I didn't get in that late, but I probably did have a beer too many. I can't hold my liquor like I did in my younger days."

Stella flipped the pancakes and raised the frying pan from the heat. "I figured that, too. I'm taking the kids to an early movie, that way you can rest after breakfast. You're off work tomorrow, too, right? Maybe you can cut the grass then?"

"Yeah, I can manage that-"

"Everyone," Stella announced. "Come get a plate. Grub is ready. Brandon, tell your friends you have plans today and can't play until later. Angelica, put some treats in Tux's bowl. Let's all eat with Daddy before we go to the movies. Which one do you want to see?"

Listening to his two children bicker about the various movies playing at the theater warmed Dylan's heart. Nobody was shocked that Brandon wanted to watch a superhero movie and that Angelica wanted to see a cartoon.

Stella was a great wife and in a good mood today. She was taking the kids out so that he could rest in a quiet house and shake off last night's drunk. It felt like the pancakes adsorbed some of last night's beer, and Dylan almost thought about going to the theater as a family. Almost.

Before leaving the house, Stella tucked Dylan in bed, pulling the sheet all the way to his chin. "I love you, babe," she said as she walked out the door. "I wouldn't be mad if there were a pizza here waiting for us when we got home for lunch."

Part Two: Let's Have Fun

Rude Awakening

"Dylan, wake up."

Dylan was half-asleep, and didn't hear anything other than the panic in his wife's voice, yet for some reason, she wasn't screaming. Hearing her didn't mean he had fully awakened yet to figure out her problem.

Stella's long fingernails dug into Dylan's bicep from where she had squeezed him out of fear. In a hushed tone, she asked, "Dylan, do you hear that?"

Shaking his arm free, he rose his head above his pillow and listened. "Nope. I hear nothing. Why?"

"Shhh!" she instructed. "Listen. There it is again."

"Brandon's probably getting a soda. Or maybe Tux wanted to go outside. I'm sure it's nothing."

'No...," she extended a pause as she held a finger in the air. "There it is again."

There was no denying what sounded like a man's voice, followed by a woman's, coming from the kitchen.

"Where's the gun?" Stella asked, still whispering.

"I'm sure it's the TV or something," Dylan said not-so-confidently. "We don't need the gun. Don't you remember telling me to put it in the safe? In the basement?"

"Yeah, but after twenty years of marriage, I've learned you don't do everything I ask of you. Never in a timely manner. This is the one time you actually chose to hear me? Great."

"I'm sure it's nothing, honey," Dylan noted, still unsure of himself, stood carefully, trying to be as quiet as possible and slipped on his pajama bottoms. "Listen," now it was his turn to raise his finger in the air. "Is that Tux's paws on the hardwood floor?"

"If Tux is downstairs," Stella said as she jumped out of the bed, her voice getting louder with each word, "then that means that Angelica is down here, too."

Being parents of small children, they knew better than to sleep fully nude, but Stella's silk camisole and boy shorts didn't leave much to the imagination. Not worried about her modesty, the worried mother swung open the bedroom door and darted down the hallway.

Even though he tried to be as fast as his wife, Dylan fell short and couldn't move as quickly. Watching his wife turn the corner and enter the kitchen wasn't as bad as what he heard her say, loudly.

"Who are you?"

Next, what sounded like a gunshot boomed through the home.

Breath no longer existed in Dylan's lungs. His ears heard nothing for the next second. His jaw fell open, but there were no words.

There was one goal, and it was to check on Stella and his children.

There was no logic in running towards a room where there was possibly an intruder, who probably had a gun, but it was the only reaction Dylan's fragile mind could muster.

This was his home. His family. His job was to be the protector and if what he assumed was happening was really happening, then he had failed at his job.

It might have only been a fraction of a second, or maybe a few seconds, Dylan wasn't sure, but he turned the corner to see Stella, standing in the dark, dropping to her knees.

"You bitch! You shot my dog!"

Hearing Stella speak was a good sign that she wasn't shot dead on the spot.

In Stella's hands was a reddened Tux. What was once white fur was now matted fur, sticky with crimson.

Priorities had always been important to Dylan, but at this moment those no longer existed. The only thing his mind could focus on was his family. His brain didn't register the two strangers, man and woman, standing on the far side of his kitchen. "Stella, are you okay?"

Her head moved almost in slow motion, her eyes never leaving Tux, but her head turned towards her husband. "Poor Tux! She shot Tux!"

The word 'she' was what got Dylan's attention. It would have been logical thinking that if Tux had been shot, then there must have been an intruder with a gun. However, Dylan couldn't process thought, nevertheless rationalize logic. "She who?"

It took himself saying the words out loud for it to strike him that there was someone else in the room with them.

Silently the female intruder raised her right hand, palm outward and wiggled her fingers. The wave was almost friendly. "She me." With her other arm, she raised a weapon, specifically a sawed-off double barreled shotgun.

His mind scrambled, but Dylan looked at Tux once again. If the woman had shot Tux with such a messy weapon, then the small dog would have been blown to bits. Tux was dying, possibly dead by now, but there was clearly one hole in the center of the dog's throat. *Does she have a handgun, too? Or is there someone else here?*

It was nerves, but Dylan's eyes blinked repeatedly as he searched the dark room for another person. A man, large in stature, with a black ski mask showing only his eyes and mouth, stepped forward and waved. "Actually, he, I, shot the dog." The man must have been proud of his statement because he stopped waving, and pointed to himself.

"What do you want?" Dylan asked as he instinctively lowered himself to the floor and wrapped his arms around his hysterical wife.

Stella cradled Tux, rocking the canine corpse back and forth.

"Who are you? Why are you here?"

The female had a high-pitched voice and sounded like a squawking parrot. "We like to have fun. We were bored. Thought we could have some fun here?"

The man was so tall that when he nodded, it almost looked like he would hit his head on the ceiling.

It was hard to decipher in the dark whether the man was plump or muscular, but Dylan's instincts kicked in and he was weighing the options on how he would defend his family against two armed intruders. "Money? You want money? I'll pay you to go away."

The male intruder stepped forward. Moonlight from the window confirmed the muscles bulging from the sides of his neck and his arms. "Why do they always think we'll leave if they give us money? We'll take the money and have fun with them. Both." His baritone voice echoed off the walls.

"Tux is dead!" Stella exclaimed over her sobbing. "Tux is dead!"

Thinking out loud did Dylan no favors. "If Tux is down here, where's Angelica?"

"Is that your daughter?" a squeaky voice asked.

"What? Yeah."

"Her and the boy both are fine, for now," the deep voice stated with authority. "Now, let's have fun. In the bedroom."

The way they both raised their weapons made it clear they weren't asking, and that it was an offer that Dylan couldn't refuse.

"Stella, baby, put Tux down. Stand up with me, we have to go in the other room. We have to do this for Angelica and Brandon."

It was like controlling a puppet, but Stella easily moved as Dylan led her to the bedroom. Her legs did what they were supposed to, but it was her face that was a giveaway that her mind was elsewhere. Gone. Not with her for now.

Intro to Fun

"Stella," Dylan said as he sat his wife on the edge of the bed. The ruffled blankets beneath her didn't seem to make her uncomfortable. "Baby, c'mon. Listen to me. I need you. The kids need you."

"Ain't they so sweet?" the female invader asked the man that towered over her. "Why don't ya ever talk like that to me?"

Hearing those words angered the masked man, causing him to grunt loudly. Coming through the ski mask distorted the noise, making the man an intimidating monstrosity. "You!" he growled as pointed the handgun at Dylan. "Quit making me look bad. I'll kill you, or a kid, right now."

"Where are my children?"

The smile, the way the woman's lips disappeared beneath the mouth hole of the ski mask, made it clear that she would take pleasure in answering that question. "They're asleep. We snuck into their rooms, gave them a little something something to help them sleep, and took their phones and computers. And we left a babysitter up there."

"A little something something? What does that mean? They're young. Drugs could irreparably damage their nervous systems. Who's up there with my children?"

The large man held up his handgun, silver and shining in the light. "This could hurt them worse."

"Dylan," Stella muttered under her breath. "Dylan, don't let them hurt my babies."

Relieved, Dylan finally found a reason to smile. "You're back. You're here, with me? I need you right now."

"Yeah, yeah," the squawking female said. "I'm ready. Let's have fun. Who loves who the most?"

"What does that mean?"

"Me and my man," the slender, masked woman started explaining, "you can call me Elle, and him Jay. Jay and I like to have fun and see if we love each other enough. Let's call this a test of your love for each other, our own personal test."

The words made no sense in Dylan's fragile mind. "I'm not a marriage counselor. My wife isn't either. We don't even know you. We can't help you with that. I don't-"

The gruff voice from the man now known as Jay was enough to stop Dylan from speaking. "Don't backtalk. We have guns. We will use them. Let Elle explain."

After taking a bow, as if she were a performer on a stage in front of an audience, Elle continued. "Yeah, we might get married soon, but we're curious if we love each other enough. So we're going to test you two. How long have you been married?"

"Going on twenty years."

Dylan was relieved that his wife was coherent and speaking, and squeezed her hand for comfort.

Using the short shotgun, Elle waved it between the married couple. "So you have to love each other a lot. Like a whole lot. Jay's afraid I love him more than he loves me. He's scared he'll hurt me in the long run."

"As much as I appreciate this history, I don't see what you're getting at. I'll pay you to leave," Dylan offered.

"Shut up!" Jay intervened. "Don't interrupt my old lady!"

"Well, I told Jay that love is pain. Hey, you," Elle used the weapon as a pointer and got Stella's attention. "Who loves who more? You love him more or he loves you more?"

"I love Dylan more, no doubt."

"Don't say that, Stella! You know that's not true. Anyway, you don't know what they'll do to us, depending on our answers."

With a chuckle, Elle lowered her weapon. "This will be fun. You ready, Jay?"

The mountain of a man stepped back and raised his handgun, aimed towards the bed.

Elle sat her weapon on the dresser, sure that her man had everything under control. She left the room, leaving behind an eerie silence. Dylan eyed the shotgun, but knew there was no way he could leap across the room without Jay putting a bullet in him.

Moments later, Elle returned, carrying a large black bag.

The sound of her quickly unzipping it made Dylan cringe in fear, knowing that soon its contents would be revealed. "You already have guns? Why do you need more weapons?"

Slowly, the woman held up a butcher knife, which appeared much larger in contrast to her petite arm. "Nope. Not this one yet." She continued to dig around the black bag, and now it was audible that metal on metal was clanging together. "This is the one I want." With a flick of her wrist, something small and shiny was tossed onto the bed."

"Scissors? Tiny scissors? What's that for?" Dylan's mind was going crazy with possibilities. "I don't understand."

"Someone is going to lose a finger. Not me. Not Jay. One of you two. The question is who loves who more?

Who's willing to take the pain, and who's willing to gift the pain?"

Small Fun

After a long laugh, Elle elaborated. "I believe pain is truth. Real. Not always bad. So I'm gonna show my man just that."

The gulp Dylan took moved his Adam's apple and it jumped in his throat. "You're crazy. That doesn't make any sense. This is nonsense."

"Dylan, he has a gun aimed at your head. What's a finger compared to a bullet? What else are we supposed to do? Here," Stella shivered with fear as she held out her hand. "Cut mine off. The smallest one."

"No." The word escaped Dylan's lips before he even had time to think. "I wouldn't hurt you. Never like that."

"Sixty seconds!" Jay growled. "Think fast!"

"Just get it over with, Dylan. I love you that much."

"Babe, I love you and the kids enough to die for you. You think I'd cut off your finger? No way. Cut mine off."

His hand was trembling, but he held it out in front of him. With his other hand, he picked up the scissors and placed them in his wife's hands.

Stella tried to recoil her arm and not hold the sharp cutters, but she glanced at the gun pointed at her. "They're so small. They're surgical scissors. Right? I can't do this. It's not right."

Now, Elle mocked her like a cheerleader, complete with wiggling her arms and kicking her legs. "Do it! Do it! Do it!"

"Do it, Stella! Now!" Dylan demanded. "Please. I don't want them to hurt you or the kids."

"How sweet is that, Jay? That's love. He loves her enough to hurt. Like I love you enough, even if you hurt me. You got it?"

"I do, honey bunny." Sweet words coming from the muscular man's mouth sounded foreign.

"If I may," Elle interjected. "I prefer the ring finger, left hand. Below the wedding ring."

Dylan nodded as he looked at his left hand.

"What if we use a tourniquet around his wrist, before we do it?" Stella queried. "I guarantee it'll still hurt him, but I don't want him to bleed out."

"Are you a doctor?" asked the large man.

"No. Far from it. A pharmacist, but that's common sense."

Elle rattled her head around as a sign that she was deep in thought. "I'll allow it."

Jay handed them a belt from the top of the dresser, and Stella got to work wrapping it around her husband's wrist, hoping it would prevent some blood loss.

Dylan tried to offer words of comfort to his wife. "Baby, you're shaking so bad. You can do this. You have to be strong, for the kids. No matter what, I promise that I'll still love you after this. Maybe even more than I do now. Maybe they'll leave after this."

The two intruders looked at each other lovingly as the married couple shared a moment of staring into each other's eyes.

"This is what I'm talking about," Elle broke the silence. "Get on with it. We'll talk after the deed is done."

Moisture leaked from Dylan's eyes even though they were closed tight. While he was waiting for the pain, Stella placed his hand across her thigh, leveraging his finger in the gap between her legs. The warmth from her skin was small solace.

To offset the small heat, the short blades of the scissors were cold as he felt them around his finger. The scraping of the sharp object on his wedding ring made his teeth hurt. There was nothing that could have prepared him for what was to come.

She wasn't gentle about it as Stella squeezed her hand and brought the blades together, and they did more than break the top layers of flesh, but didn't do much more than that.

Reflexes kicked in and Dylan tried to move his hand away from the affliction, but his wife held him tight around the tourniquet.

"Don't move. I'm trying the best I can, these blades are so short," Stella commented. "Are you okay?"

Through gritted teeth, Dylan answered. "Just do it. Fast!"

She tried again, this time pressing the sharp sides of the blades into the pre-existing wound. Instead of doing one squeeze of the scissors' finger holds, she brought them together multiple times, moving as she did, going deeper, until they struck bone. "There's bone there! These won't cut the bone!"

"Maybe not, but if you move it around, you'll find the tendons and such. Cut around the bone. Between finger bone and hand bone," Jay instructed, speaking from experience. "You'll find a weak spot. It can happen."

Unsure which was worse, the agony or the conversation, Dylan tried to still himself. Like a wounded animal, Dylan growling under his breath. "It's. Okay. Baby. Just. Do. It."

Her hands were shaking badly, so that made it worse for Stella as she tried to discover the weak zone that Jay spoke of. The blades wiggled between the wedding band and metacarpophalangeal joint.

Crimson liquid dripped, staining her thighs and the bed sheet, but it wasn't as much of a flow if she hadn't used a tourniquet.

His eyes were still closed, but Dylan didn't need to be looking when the scissors dissected the area for which they were searching. It was a new suffering. A pop beneath his skin as a tendon was severed. Like a snapped rubber band springing in two different directions.

Stella felt her husband try to pull away from the danger, but calmly, she spoke to him. "We're over halfway finished. Almost there."

Trying his best not to lose consciousness, Dylan thought of his family's safety. "Just. Do. It."

His wife continued with her project and after three more snips, she felt the digit fall upon her thigh, heavy with the ring. "All done. It's over, baby. It's over."

It was when Dylan opened his eyes and saw his mutilated hand that he started to hyperventilate. Between deprived breaths, he tried to form words, but it was nothing more than sounds. "It's okay. It's okay."

The bystanders weren't sure if he was trying to convince himself or his wife.

Questions

"He's not bleeding bad," Jay said with a chuckle. "Get him a bandage. He'll be alright."

"Eh," Elle squeaked out. "We'll get to that, in a minute. I want to see something. How's it feel, Dylan?"

By this time, Dylan was lying with his head in Stella's lap, the blood from her thighs marking his cheek. "Huh? It hurts. How do you think it feels?"

Not very appreciative that someone was being flippant towards his girl, Jay stepped forward, the weapon inches from Dylan's face. "Don't be like that. She doesn't mean physically. You know what she means."

Dylan's internal dialogue was busy trying to figure out how he was supposed to know that. His wounded hand was perched atop his side, crimson running down his chest. "I don't know what she means. I feel like you're crazy. We've done what you asked. Just leave now. Please."

The way Stella was running her fingers through Dylan's hair was more habit than an act of compassion. "Yeah. Maybe you should go now."

"Wait a minute!" Jay protested. "Let Elle speak! Dang. Screaming is too hot in this mask," he said as he removed the covering from his face.

"Yeah, I'll take mine off, too. It's better without this on. Do you still love your wife? Someone that hurt you so bad."

Dylan was more focused on the fact that the monsters in his house were now naked on their faces. Their appearance had been exposed. A movie once taught him that if the criminal allows you to see their face, that they intend to kill you so that you can't identify them. "Of course, I love my wife. I'll always love my wife. I won't stop loving her because two psychos forced her to injure me."

Elle had been holding the severed digit, the finger bloody and turning blue. She fiddled with it, watching it roll between her fingers like it was the most interesting thing she had ever seen. "What's the worst pain you've ever gifted your wife?"

"What? I've never. I would never hit her, or cut her. Not only that, but I've never even pushed her. I love her!"

"Jay's a man. Worried about hurting me. Like hurting my emotions. Look at this, right here," she tapped her fingernail against the wedding ring. "This changes everything. After a wedding, a man is supposed to be faithful. Only have sex with one woman for the rest of his life. Do you think's that normal? Is that natural? When you married Stella, did your dick stop getting hard when you saw other women?"

As off-putting as the question was, the gun motivated Dylan to answer. "It's not your business. But it's not about a man's... uh...er..." his mind scrambled for the correct term. "It's not about the man's sexual organs. It's about trust, honesty, and loyalty. Once again, we're not marriage counselors. Please. Leave now. Someone else could help you better."

"Is that so?" Elle continued. "You've been married a long time. Have you been faithful? Or have you had fun on the side?"

"What? I don't see what this has to do with anything."

Stella's fingers stopped rubbing Dylan's hair. "Why didn't you answer her? It should be an easy answer."

Dylan didn't have to see her eyes to hear the hurt in her voice. "Stella, you know how much I love you and our family. You and the kids are my whole world. The issue right now is getting these people out of our home!"

"I'm a bit proud of the little man," Jay intervened. "He's lost a finger. His integrity could be compromised, yet he finds a way to skirt the issue. You want us gone? Answer Elle's questions. Honestly."

Between pain and the revelation that the intruders were probably going to kill them, Dylan didn't know how to answer. "What do you want to hear, Elle? That men cheat, but that doesn't mean whether they love their wives?"

Proudly, Elle leaned in closer to her victim, sure of her safety. "No, Dyyyyllllllllaaaaan." Exaggerating his name made her smile. "I want to know if you've been faithful. You're not answering, so I'll ask her. Stella. Has your husband ever cheated on you?"

The dryness of Stella's mouth was obvious from her speech, the way her tongue tried to lick the roof of her mouth for saliva. "I don't know. I don't think so, but he didn't answer you. There was a time a few years ago, I smelled perfume on him after he went to a bar, but he said the waitress had to lean over him to reach the far end of the table to refill beer."

"You believed him?" Elle's eyebrows raised as she expressed surprise. "Honey, are you dumb or something? Dylan, three seconds. Answer honestly, or I'll go upstairs and I'll-"

"Okay! Okay! Maybe! Just once or twice!" After the words fell from his mouth, Dylan was shocked with his response. "Stella, I'm saving the kids here. Don't think about any of this."

"No! I want the truth! We've been married so long and I have a right to know!"

"Stella, I've lost a finger. I won't lose you and the kids, too. This isn't the time for this."

"See, Jay," Elle remarked. "This is why we're here. Is married life for us? Maybe they can work it out, just like we could, if one of us ever cheated."

"You're running around sticking your dick in everything that moves? And I'm the one in the wrong?" Stella's accusation was powerful. Quickly, she shifted her body weight, removing Dylan's head from her lap. "Is getting your dick wet worth it?"

"Baby, do you realize our situation right now?"

Jay leaned back on the dresser, relaxing the gun to his side. "I agree with him. He said it happened once or twice. Not in everything that moves. And I believe him. I mean, we threatened to kill his kids. The threat of that seems to bring out honesty."

"Shhh," Elle placed a finger over her lips. "Let them work this out. I want to see how it plays out."

Answers?

As Stella stood and moved to the far side of the bed, Jay stood back at attention, no longer relaxed, like a watchdog.

"Who was she? Who were they?"

Trying to sit up caused Dylan's hand to throb. "It doesn't matter. Look around. We need to think of the kids."

"It does matter," Elle said with a nod. "I want to see if she can forgive you. To see how it would end up with me and Jay."

Her flimsy logic made Dylan's stomach turn. "They were nobody. Never a relationship. Mostly strippers. Just blowing off steam," Dylan answered, ashamed of himself.

"Strippers? Like with diseases? What if you gave me herpes or something?"

"I always used a condom!"

"Why them? Why not me?"

"You're tired a lot. It means nothing!"

Elle's neck flipped like a swivel watching their conversation, very much like watching a tennis match. She turned towards Jay and whispered. "I wish we had popcorn." After making her voice louder, she turned her attention to Stella. " Stella, can you forgive him? It looks like he forgave you for cutting off his finger. Can you do the same?"

"You forced me to cut off his finger!" Stella's displaced anger, wrath meant for her husband, was now honed in on the maniacs with guns.

"Baby," Dylan said gently. "Calm down. Everything will be okay. Keep cool. We need to survive this."

"Before you stuck it in those hookers, did you think about me? How much it would hurt me?"

"Stella," Dylan glanced around the room and saw that Jay and Elle were relaxed and watching them, like they were on display and a form of entertainment. His thoughts were that if he kept this up, maybe they'd relax enough for him to make a move and get a gun. " This isn't the time or place. Of course, I thought of you. But I assure you it didn't hurt you worse than losing a finger. They meant nothing to me. It was only a physical action on my part."

"What!" Stella responded to her husband's choice of the wrong words. "Losing a finger hurts worse than finding out your husband is a cheat? A liar? I don't even know you anymore!"

"Yes, you do, baby. I'm the same man. The one who would do anything for my family."

"So you got your dick wet for your family? How bad would it hurt to lose your cock?"

"Don't even play. Don't give them ideas. And I didn't say that."

"This is better than the movies," Jay whispered to Elle. "But I think I like him. He's not so bad."

"He's a cheater and you say he's not so bad?" Elle barked back. "What's wrong with you?"

"He didn't have relationships. It was an act. Animals have sex. Dogs have sex. It's a physical need. Not a sign of love."

Jay and Elle's argument got heated and louder than the married couple's debate.

Everyone stared at each other and the room fell silent.

"I feel bad for the little dude," Jay said as he dug into his pocket, and pulled out a butane torch lighter. After he flung it on the bed, he gave Dylan some advice. "Put the flame to your finger stump. It'll stop bleeding."

The look on Dylan's face was more questioning Jay's sanity, but knew it was solid advice. It would hurt, but would be better than losing even more blood. Also, the tourniquet had cut off most of the blood flow to his entire hand. The pins and needles numb feeling was getting annoying. It was the threat of more pain that gave Dylan caution. "The tourniquet is doing its job. I'm not bleeding too badly."

"Yeah, you should cauterize the wound, remove the tourniquet, get the blood flow back in your hand," Stella said with a sneer. "I'll do it, if you won't."

This piqued Elle's interest. "For a pharmacist, you seem very knowledgeable. Are you offering to help him? Or do you want to do it and hurt your husband even more?"

"To hurt me," Dylan said in a low voice. "Open flame would damage more tissue. Cauterization requires some sort of conduit. Like getting metal hot, and then applying the warmed metal to the wound. Stella wants me to hurt more. If it'll make you feel better, go ahead, babe. I love you enough for you to take your frustrations out on me."

"That's true love," Elle whispered to Jay.

With his baritone voice, it was almost impossible for Jay to whisper. "I agree. I told you, I like him."

Deeper Wounds

"It's for your own good," Stella declared as she flipped the lid on the torch lighter and pressed the button. A blue and orange flame ejected from the device with an audible whooshing sound.

Staring in his wife's eyes made Dylan question himself as to why he was holding his hand out for his wife to injure him deeper. All he saw was disdain, distrust, and contempt. "If you think this will fix us, I'm more than willing. Get on with it then."

The fire hadn't been on his finger nub for a full second before he jerked his hand backwards. "Oh no! Oh no!"

"Don't be a baby," Stella teased. "Let me do it."

"See, Elle, I like him, maybe more than I like her."

Jay's remark made Stella's head turn quickly. "What did you say? You think it's okay for him to cheat on me?"

"I didn't say that. But I do see that he loves you."

Inspecting his hand took all of Dylan's attention. The combination of pain and stress made it hard to focus. Black, mixed with dried, burnt blood, were the new colors of the tip of the small protuberance from his hand. Toppled with the offending aroma of burnt flesh (and possibly hair), Dylan feared he would vomit. "If I do this, allow you to do this, will that prove how much I love you? How much I'm willing to hurt to make you feel better for my hurting you?"

She didn't have to think about it. Stella nodded. "Yeah, sure would. For starters."

Extending his arm for her to inflict more pain on him was Dylan's way of extending a symbol of peace to his wife. It may have been a disfigured symbol, but a symbol all the same.

Stella didn't need another invitation. Acting quick was her reaction as she clicked the flame and brought it to his hand again.

Dried blood on the edges of the opened flesh bubbled and popped, releasing blackened blood particles into the air. It was small and quick, he didn't hold his hand to her pain for more than three seconds, but as his arm retreated, she followed him with the flame.

As he brought his hand close to his chest, the flame was close enough to singe the hairs of his pectoral region. In slow motion, he could practically watch what was once curled hair slowly withdraw, like it was trying to get back inside of his body.

Dylan's cries howled inside his head like echos. Then he vomited and fell sideways on the bed. Strings of saliva and last night's dinner clung to his chin, tethering his face to the clumps of stomach bile his stomach had up heaved. The vulgar smell of the upchucked food did him no favors with his queasiness.

"Is he passed out?" Elle asked. "What fun is this?"

"Hold up," Stella said with an attitude. "What's this about liking him more than me? I don't think you understand-"

The fearful husband wasn't fully unconscious and it clicked in his mind that his wife's mouth would get her into deep trouble, so he cut her off abruptly, screaming in pain once again. "I'm not passed out! I'll do anything and everything to save my family!"

"Oh, you're awake. Anything you say?" Stella inquired, sounding more angry than concerned for her husband.

"I'm not well. I've lost a finger, you've burned my hand, and now I'm sick. Spewing chunks. But sure, let's forget about the psychos in our house, threatening our children. Let's work out our own marital issues. Right here, right now." Sarcasm was hard to pull off while gritting his teeth through pain, but Dylan made his point very clear.

"Stella," Jay growled to get her attention. "How much do you love your husband? What if we turned the tables on you?"

"On me? Why? How? That wouldn't be right?"

"Yeah, I'm curious, too," Elle said as she took Jay's handgun and now pointed it towards the angry wife. "Babe, why don't you dig through the bag of toys? Find something for Dylan to do to Stella, then see how she feels."

Turned Around and Redirected

"I do love my husband!" Stella objected. "I have a right to be mad at him. I can do both. Love him and be mad. Why do I need to be hurt to prove that?"

"Okay," Jay said as he stood after digging through the black bag. "Pruning shears. Should be easy to do with one hand. Would you still love your husband after he removes one of your nipples?"

Lying down made it hard for Dylan to reach for the tool with his good hand, so he sat up. "You want me to hurt my wife? I can't do that. You'd have to shoot me before I did that." The blades of the pruning shears were small, but that didn't prevent him from trying to devise a way to attack the invaders. Eventually, his mind told him it was pointless. Pruning shears, especially with a busted hand, would be no good against two people with guns.

"He's getting me kind of hot," Elle squealed in her high-pitch voice. "How sweet is that? He loves her that much. I'm really impressed with him."

The following noise was deafening.

A loud boom, mixed with the smell of gunpowder.

Shattering of the mirror on the wall behind the bed.

Multiple senses were distressed.

Elle screamed. "Uh oh! My bad!"

She and Jay both got a good laugh out of this.

Dylan eyed his wife up and down. 'You okay? Are you shot?"

"No."

"I don't think I was either," he replied, thinking it would comfort his wife. Instead, she stared down the female intruder.

"What was that? Because I don't want Dylan to cut off my nipple?"

"No, my finger slipped. A complete accident."

"What if you had been pointing the weapon upwards?" Dylan accused. "It could have shot one of my children upstairs."

"But it wasn't, and it didn't. I'm sorry."

An apology coming from the intruder took some of the edge off, and Dylan saw what he hoped would be a way into her head. If only he could play into her humanity and maybe get some sympathy, then maybe they'd leave. "If you leave now, I won't tell anyone. I'll say I lost my finger working on the lawn mower or something. We have children. Young children. They mean everything to me."

"That's not happening, but here's what will happen," Elle wiggled her finger while pointing at the pruning shears. "I'm giving you the grand opportunity to get even with your wife. Cut off her nipple."

"I refuse. I won't do it."

'He really does love her. She doesn't deserve him if you ask me."

"Jay!" Elle warned. "Keep your comments to yourself."

"We're the ones with the guns. I feel like I can say whatever I want to say."

"My shirt's already off," Dylan said, leaning close to his wife. "Cut off my nipple. They want to see bloodshed. Let's give it to them."

There was zero hesitation. Stella grabbed the tool and pressed the silver blades to her husband's chest. His brown budded nipple looked so small in comparison to the angry tool that was threatening to cut off a part of his body.

Same as she did with the scissors on his now amputated finger, she squeezed the handle of the tool.

The blades came together, easily slicing off the teat. Like a flimsy pencil eraser that had been applied to a piece of paper too hard, the small lump of body tissue disconnected from his body. A trickle of blood leaked like a tiny stream navigating Dylan's body hair, towards his navel, where it began to collect like a tiny pool of scarlet.

"It's okay, baby," Dylan stared in his wife's eyes. "It's okay. This doesn't hurt nearly as bad as my finger."

"You deserve this. You deserve everything you get."

"I know you're mad at me right now, but look at the bigger picture. Think of Brandon and Angelica."

"Yeppers," Ella agreed, waving the gun in the air. "We're the bigger picture."

More Trials and Tribulations

"And you say that didn't hurt?"

Dylan was shocked by his wife's question. The two hoodlums, standing in his bedroom, with guns and the bag full of torture devices, seemed entertained. They were now relaxed and watching the married couple like they were performers on a television set.

Dylan's hope was that Stella was noticing how Elle and Jay were not as threatening as they had been and was playing into their games, so that maybe he might get a chance to grab a gun and fight back.

"If you say that didn't hurt, then it most certainly didn't hurt as bad as finding out that my husband has had affairs."

"Not affairs. Just a couple flings. I'm so sorry."

"No. I've suspected this for a while. There were two times that you told me you were out with Dave, but I know because his wife told me, he came home three hours before you. And there was the perfume smell a long time ago…"

"Stella, baby," Dylan begged with a wink, hoping she understood that he was trying to distract the intruders. "I'm so sorry. What can I do for you to forgive me?"

"Let me hurt you, as much as you hurt me."

"What? Are you serious?"

"Now we're talking," Jay intervened. "But I'm for him hurting her."

"Me too," Elle chimed in. " If it came down to brass tacks, I'd say Dylan loves her more."

"No, don't disregard my wife like that," Dylan pleaded. "She has a good heart. She's a woman. She's angry, is all, and rightfully so."

"No, I don't get it," Jay disagreed. "We're men. Our cocks have a mind of their own. So what? Love and sex are two different things."

"And that's why you won't marry me?"

This was good. The intruders were now having their own conversation, not watching their victims on the bed. Closely and attentively, Dylan watched for an opening, hoping in his head that one of them would get so mad that one of them would leave the room, making the act of saving his family much easier.

"I'll marry you," Jay said with sincerity, "but honestly, I'd probably fool around behind your back."

"Now we're back to square one, and I'm not happy. Not happy at all." Elle expressed her unhappiness with an exaggerated frown.

Dylan felt for the large man who was being honest with his girlfriend. Whoever said that the truth is always best had never tried to keep a woman happy.

"Great, my woman isn't happy," Jay scowled. "Let's get back to it. Let's see what's in the bag."

The item he produced was larger than the last two. "Dylan, if I entrust you with this nail gun, can I be sure you won't shoot me or Elle with it? Just shoot your wife. Put a three-inch nail somewhere in Stella's body. Where you put it is your choice. Anywhere."

Dylan had to compose himself. A nail gun wasn't a gun that shot bullets, but maybe he could do something to help his family. Before he had a chance to answer, Stella did.

"Give it to me! I won't shoot you. And I'll put the nail in his penis!"

"Yeah, I like her again," Elle said, taking the tool that was repurposed as a weapon. "I'll give it to her. You got a problem with that?"

Jay frowned again. "Yeah, I do. I'm a man, too, and won't allow any metal anywhere near his penis."

Elle argued. "He cheated on her. He deserves this. Maybe I'd do the same to you if you cheated."

With his eyes, Jay practically apologized to Dylan, with a sincere glance and turned away, shaking his head.

"Wait, Stella," Dylan had to try to talk his wife out of this. "Think this through. This would damage me sexually for the rest of my life and-"

"You deserve it."

Wounded Pride and Manhood

"I won't stand for this!" Jay was outraged. "This is too much!"

As good as it felt having an ally on his side, Dylan wasn't sure how this would play out. Did that mean the male intruder was turning on his accomplice or on Stella? If Jay was turning against Elle, that would help Dylan try to fight back and escape.

If Jay was turning against Stella, her life could be in danger.

There was still the possibility that there was a third person upstairs with his children. Dylan highly doubted that after Elle accidentally discharged her weapon. If someone had been upstairs, wouldn't they have come downstairs to see what happened?

"I'll allow it," Elle stated. "Let's see if he loves his wife after that."

"I know you, and you'll do what you want. That doesn't mean I have to stand here and watch it," Jay said as he left the room, taking the shotgun with him. Before passing the door threshold, he gave his girlfriend some advice. "Keep the handgun trained on whoever has the nail gun. Even if they did shoot you, you probably wouldn't die, and if you scream, I'll be here in two seconds to blow their head off."

While Dylan was busy calculating in his head whether he could take the both of them out with a nail gun, the women got to talking.

"I'm not stupid!" Stella exclaimed. "I'll shoot my husband's pecker. Not you."

"No!" Dylan objected. "Let me shoot my wife!" His logic was that he would never hurt his wife, but if he got the shot right, and placed a nail in Elle's eye, maybe it would kill her instantly. Then maybe he could grab her weapon and take out Jay also. There were many 'IFS" and "MAYBES" in that scenario, but it was only his only hope right now.

"Sorry, Dylan, I trust her more than you."

Defeated by Elle's words, Dylan tried again. "What if I promise not to hurt you?"

"You'll promise? That changes everything… Not! Do I look stupid to you?"

Everything was happening so fast. Stella now had the nail gun in her hands. "Take off your pants."

"Please, Stell, think this through," he hoped using his wife's pet name would soften her heart. Then he hushed his voice. "Think this through. Give it to me. I'll fight our way out of here."

"Take off your pants!"

Every fiber of Dylan's being was hopeful that his wife had her own plan, that she would help them get out of this situation. It appeared that Elle was engrossed in their transaction, so Dylan played along.

There was no shame in his nudity as he stood to remove the clothing from the lower half of his body. The standing position was the perfect opportunity to try and get a jump on Elle. If only he had the nail gun.

Swiftly, Dylan reached for the weapon his wife was holding, but she pulled it away from him. Hearing the click of Elle cocking her handgun gave him pause, and he lifted both hands above his head, a sign of surrender and that he was not a threat to her.

His vulnerable position was the perfect time for Stella to act. She neared the nail gun to his penis, and pulled the trigger.

Whoosh. Whoosh.

Two nails ejected from the machine, both in rapid succession.

Dylan fell to his knees in immense pain.

Since his penis had been flaccid and dangling loosely between his legs, the forceful impact bent his member backwards, where the nail also pierced his scrotum, the head of the nail only stopping when hitting the posterior scrotum tissue wall. The second nail clinked into the first nail, blasting it completely through his body, the round nail head tearing a hole through the most sensitive parts of Dylan's body.

Reflexes kicked in and Dylan's hands reached for his man parts, as if holding them would stop the pain. The feel of warm blood coated his hands, and Dylan went into shock, wailing like a banshee.

His world went black as he fell unconscious.

Part Three: Past the Point of No Return

No Hope

Dylan woke with Jay standing between his legs.

"It's like a cock ring, even though it's a hair tie. It's wrapped around the base of his cock and his ball sack, similar to a tourniquet. The problem is that now is what's left of his dick is turning blue. Guess it's not getting any blood flow. And for real, looking at this makes my own dude parts hurt. It's like looking at a hot dog that had been boiled too long and ran over by a car. It's split, ripped, has a large hole in it. His cock is in tethers. Ribbons. I don't know if I'd want to live after this. Not after losing my cock. Patches of loose skin just drooping between his thighs. Just wrong. It's hard to tell the cock from the balls. It's all ruined meat mixed together."

Jay's husky voice was pulling Dylan out of his slumber.

"I bet he doesn't cheat on me again," Stella said with pride.

"Stella, I won't. Never again. I promise."

"Ladies and gentlemen," Elle said with excitement, "he's alive and awake. Jay, you might have saved his life. He was bleeding bad, lost tons of blood. Here's the real question. Do you still love your wife now?"

"Of course I do," Dylan muttered, soft and low. "I'll always love her."

"He's an idiot," Stella interrupted. "He can't love me if he cheated on me."

"Yes, I can. You and the kids are my everything. We've done everything you asked. Will you leave now? I need a doctor bad."

"Dr. Jay patched you up. I don't know if we're finished yet," Elle remarked. "What do ya think, Jay, Stella. Are we done?"

"Let me get the little man an ice pack or something," Jay offered with sympathy for the extreme wound. "Give him a minute."

"Let him bleed out for all I care!" Stella screamed.

"No, Stell, don't talk like that. They'll kill all of us, including the kids. They're obviously crazy."

"Here's what I don't get, Dylan," Elle began. "How can you still love her? She doesn't care if you're in pain, or if you live or die."

"I vowed to love my wife for better and worse. She's just mad at me. I'm sure we can work out our differences."

"Differences?" Stella scoffed. "That's what you call this? I call it, you were cheating and being a man whore."

"That's real marriage, real love," Jay declared. "I'd still love you, babe, if you went off on me like that. I think he's proved his love for her, no matter what he did with other women."

"I'm starting to agree with you," Elle said softly as she ran a finger across his cheek. "I love you so much."

It was hard for Dylan to focus his vision from seeing double, but from where he laid in the floor, he saw that neither psychopath was holding their weapons. If only he could bring himself to his feet and attack them. Even sitting up made him nauseous, so he knew it wasn't going to happen.

Dylan's other plan was to play into their game. Give them a show. "Stell, can't you see how much I love you? What you've done to me doesn't change that."

"This is pathetic!" Stella's voice exploded with wrath. "You have them convinced that you love me, even after your whores and hookers and strippers? I'm not buying it. Not one bit. You're a liar. You lie through your teeth!"

"I speak the truth. It hurts so bad. I really need help here."

"Give me a pair of wire pliers," Stella extended her hand.

"Well, this has turned into her game," Elle backed away from Jay and rummaged through the bag. "Let's see how long until he caves and gives up."

The thought of this being a game made Dylan resort to his last tactic. Silent prayer to a God that he wasn't even sure if he believed in. Being desperate meant that he would try anything to save his life and his family.

Can't Lie Through Your Teeth

Stella straddled her husband on the floor, and Dylan had no more fight left in him. His double vision and pain-induced-foggy-mind was making it hard for him to understand what was happening.

"Open your mouth wide!" Stella demanded.

Dylan wasn't sure what she said, and as he opened his mouth to ask her to repeat what she said, she jammed the pliers into his mouth forcefully, chipping two front teeth in the process.

The broken bits of teeth fell to the back of his throat in his downed position, causing him to open his mouth wide to try and cough them out.

The sound was internal in Dylan's head, the way the hard metal of the tool clunked onto his front tooth, attaching itself menacingly.

She was rushed, and Stella hadn't realized the tool was actually gripped onto two teeth, each a portion of half. Her hand strength wasn't the greatest, but that didn't prevent her from pulling, pushing, wiggling and jiggling the pliers.

"This looks so easy in the movies!" Stella screamed. "Why won't it come out?"

Not having the vigor to push his wife off of him made it easier on Stella, but she was still having a hard time completing her task.

The taste of copper and chunks of broken tooth assaulted Dylan's mouth.

Pain shot upwards, nerves on fire from all the way to Dylan's ears and nose.

Then, Dylan felt a snap, something came loose.

Two partial, broken teeth were cinched between the pliers, and Stella held the item above her head like a trophy. A string of saliva and blood extended like a rope, until it burst, dissipating in the air, falling into small spots of moisture.

"That's too much work. There must be an easier way. Give me a knife or something?" Stella asked.

Dylan tried to say no, but the sharp edges of his front teeth cut into the tip of his tongue, resulting in small tears of his speaking muscle.

Once again, his mouth was open and Stella struck his gingival (gum) line with a sharp point of a pocket knife. The hard substance dug into the spongy tissue, scraping bone and tooth nerves, sending more fiery sensations through the entirety of her husband's face.

Carefully, like a surgeon at work, Stella carved around the top of the broken teeth, going straight for the root. The already loosened teeth broke free from their home, spilling a release of warm blood, the fractured, unsecured portion falling to Dylan's tonsils.

"He's choking!" Jay stepped forward, shoving Stella from her husband. "Are you trying to kill him?"

Whether it was sympathy, or a man taking up for another man, something inside of Jay told him to act. The large man rolled the smaller man onto his stomach so tooth and blood would expel from his throat area.

"That's your job, right?" Stella asked. "That's the point of this, isn't it? Why shouldn't he live the last few minutes of his life in misery? Do you forget how he treated me and our marriage?"

Frothy bubbles, reddened, foamed from Dylan's face, nose and mouth as he choked and coughed. When he was turned over, the delicate, ruined area of his crotch scratched against the carpet, giving him a new hurt down below.

Dylan felt a large hand pat his back firmly, but not too hard. Knowing one of the psychopaths was rooting for him was little to no consolation.

"Dylan, quit coughing," Elle scorned. "The question is, do you still love your wife? After all of this."

Words wouldn't come out, and Dylan had a hard time hearing the question, but he nodded, thinking that was what the intruder wanted to know. Hasn't she said earlier they were testing the married couple's love? Fear struck him, frightened that if he answered wrong they would murder him or his children.

More More More

"If he enjoys sex so much, I'll give him sex," Stella announced as she now pounced on top of her husband's back, pressing him deeper into the plush carpet. She spread his butt cheeks with a grimace on her face. "What can I stick up here?"

"I can't watch this!" Jay screamed. "Elle, you have to stop this!"

"No! I'm curious to see how much he loves her!"

"He's already proved it, hasn't he?"

Stella was unhappy with Jay's train of thought. "No, he hasn't!"

"Maybe you're right, Jay. She's a mad woman right now. Dylan is getting really pale. He's lost a lot of blood."

"If you won't help me, I'll help myself," Stella stated.

As she stood, Elle and Jay both went on high guard, both grabbing for their weapons. The angry wife paid them no mind, and walked to the far side of the bed, tapping her thumb on her chin like she was deep in thought.

The not-turned-on lamp shade caught Stella's eye.

She reached her feminine hand inside, and started to unscrew a decorative lightbulb. The clear glass was shaped like an extended candle, longer than it was wide, complete with a pointed tip (opposed to the typical arbitrary bulb). Thin filament wires inside the glass broke as she shook it too hard.

"My husband likes sex, he'll get sex!"

Being prone (face down) gave Dylan a disadvantage. His body was spent, exhausted. Lying on his damaged crotch was painful, but not as painful when he tried to physically roll over. "What's happening?" His voice tired and quiet, projected into the fibers of the floor.

Jay turned away, not willing to watch. "I can't allow this, Elle. Stop it!"

"Let's see how deep his love goes. Call it an experiment."

Long fingernails scraped both buttocks, one hand on both cheeks, spreading his rear entry wide open. Blood from his penis had flowed into his crack, hardening his body hair with clotted redness.

A majority of the red liquid had pooled into the opening of his anus, mixing with the darker colors of the gluteal cleft.

Stella's audience was only herself and Elle, Dylan too weak to turn his head and Jay refusing to watch.

You could have heard a pin drop in the room due to the silence.

There was no other plan, other than to physically harm her husband.

She tried to ram the glass object inside her husband's opening, but Stella realized she had messed up after it was too late. Instead of lubing his hole and gliding the object inside, the glass shattered, a few flecks of sharpness exploding into her own fingers.

"Dammit!" Stella cursed, rising her hand to her mouth and tried to suck her own pain away.

After hearing the crunching sounds of broken glass, Jay forced himself to look, to survey the damage.

Miniscule shards of glass sparkled in the light, wedged between his buttocks, which closed into themselves after Stella removed her hands.

His butt cheeks squeezing together forced the shards deeper into the superficial tissues of his rump.

"Oh no!" Stella expressed her own pain and anger. "He's not getting off that easy!"

Now she was formulating a plan in her head and went to work collecting the sexual lubrication and another lightbulb from the very same lamp.

"He didn't even scream, Elle. Is he dead or unconscious?" Jay whispered to his partner in crime. "When do we stop this?"

"His chest is expanding, you can see it in the rib bones of his back. He's probably passed out. He's not dead if he's breathing."

Sloppy sounds of the lube being squirted on Dylan's once again spread backside ended with an air expulsion noise, meaning the tube was empty. However, there was already plenty of moisture to aid in Stella's quest of gliding the bulb Inside of her husband.

This time Stella was careful, gentle, and methodical.

Testing her excitement and moving as slow as her patience would allow, the tip of the unbroken bulb spread her husband's star-shaped opening, barely penetrating inside of Dylan's vulnerable backside.

"Slow, slow, slow," Stella spoke to herself, reminding herself to be cautious.

A third of the bulb was inside his rectum, then the tightness exploded like a small glass bomb detonating.

Once again, the glass shrapnel had also injured Stella's fingers, but it must have harmed Dylan even more.

"OWWWWWWWWW!"

"See, he's alive, I told ya," Elle teased. "Wish we'd have bet money on it."

"Yeah," Jay said quietly. "But he now has broken glass up the poop chute. When will this end?"

"Give me a few minutes with him, okay?"

Stella sat on the bed, trying to suck the pain out of her fingertips. The blood was miniscule, and the invaders agreed that she was being overly dramatic.

Elle raised her leg, shaking Dylan gently. "Hey! Do you still love her?"

When she received no response, she pulled her leg back and kicked him a bit harder. "Dylan, do you still love her?" If you don't answer me, I'll put a bullet in you, maybe even the kids. Do you still love your wife, even after she has hurt you so much?"

The words bounced around Dylan's head, pulling him from his peace of not being aware of his pain while passed out. "I love her… more than… anything… My family… means everything… to me…"

The exaggerated, slurred words, interrupted by gasps and moans, made it difficult to hear him.

"He said yes," Jay clarified. "How do you want to play this out?"

A Bad Wife

"Are you asking her or me?" Stella interrupted the intruders' private sidebar. "I say I still hurt him. Let's really test his love."

"Lady," Jay raised the shotgun and an angry vein popped out of his forehead, "I think you've taken things too far. The man is hurt plenty."

"I'll be the judge of that," Stella said. "The lightbulb didn't go deep enough. What else can I use?"

Elle offered the pliers to Stella. "What can you do with these? I'd be afraid to give you something sharp. These aren't sharp. I don't want you to kill him before my experiment ends."

She snapped the tool a couple of times, bringing the teethed part together, and Stella smiled. "I can work with these."

Quickly, she dropped to her knees on her husband's back, her body weight forcing air to escape his lungs. She spread his cheeks, amazed by what she saw. "The glass shards, they're really buried deep in his skin, but not inside of him. Not as deep as I wanted. Maybe I should try to remove some of it," Stella chuckled to herself. "It's a kindness I'll give to my husband."

She clamped the tool onto a chunk of meat, the uppermost part of the puckered star of her husband's anus. Like a child stretching putty as a game, she pulled her hand back, bringing the fatty flesh with her.

His skin stretched, his rear entry widening, to the point of no return. The majority portion sprung back in place like elastic towards his body, but a smaller portion broke, snapped and clung to the metal teeth of the tool.

As if she were a champion, Stella raised the tool above her head, awaiting her audience to congratulate her on her victory. When all she received were slack jaws, she brought the tool close to her eyes, to inspect it closely.

Using a lengthy fingernail, she scraped some of the bloody clump of body tissue from the tool. "That's not very much," she noted. "I guess I'll have to try again."

Rather than gripping the metal prongs on the exterior, she plunged the tool deeper in the rectum, which was easy due to the already in place lube and blood. When she tried to angle the pliers to get a grip on the inner rectum walls, her hand began to cramp. She pushed through her discomfort, using both hands now on the handles.

She squeezed harder, feeling the softness from preventing the jaws from clanking together. After she was sure she held a thicker chunk of meat in her grasp, she twisted the tool before pulling it out of her husband.

This time there was no visual sign of the butt tissues stretching, but she could feel it, like a slight resistance as she tugged.

There was a much larger chunk of flesh trapped between the tips of the pliers, red dripping onto Dylan's bare buttocks in splotches.

Stella tried again, trying to get a response. "Do y'all see this? Look, it's from way up in there. Why isn't there more blood then?"

"He's lying face down. Any blood would flow deeper, up the poop chute," Jay observed. "I think that's enough of that."

"I disagree, Jay," Elle said while leaning closer to get a better look at the damaged rump. "I doubt this would kill him. I'll allow it. His back is still expanding. Look at his back ribs moving. He's still breathing."

"This isn't right. The man has suffered enough."

"Enough?" Stella mocked. "He cheated on me. Do you know how bad it hurts me to know that he prefers strippers and hookers over his own wife?"

"Dylan, do you still love your wife, even after she's hurt you more?"

Elle's voice pulled Dylan from his stupor, but words seemed impossible. Knowing that his family's lives depended on him, Dylan raised his head and moved it up and down. "Yea."

Part Three: Family Time

Small Voice

"Mommy! Daddy!"

The small, male voice wafted through the house, accompanied by creaking of floorboards upstairs.

"That's Brandon!" All of a sudden, Dylan jolted into an alert position, sat up, and his mind went crazy with a million scenarios of how this could play out. "He's coming down. I bet he woke up his sister. They'll both be in the kitchen in a few minutes. They can't see Tux. Please don't hurt my children."

The house sounds of several small feet on the stairs was a clear sign that there was nobody upstairs with the children, no intruder keeping them confined to their rooms.

"Stella, you have to do something." Dylan swiveled his head to Elle. "Please, let her get our children back in bed."

'She's covered in a bit of blood. I'm not completely heartless. Throw a nightgown over your dirty clothes. I'll head them off in the kitchen so they don't see the family pet."

The thought of Elle with his children terrified Dylan.

The thought of the kids seeing Tux's corpse terrified him even more.

Stella made herself presentable and followed Elle down the hallway.

"So, it's just me and you." The way Jay said it, low and gently, made him sound halfway sympathetic to the ordeal. He reached into a chest drawer that Stella left open, and placed an oversized nightgown on the bed. "Put this on. I know you can't hide your bloodied hand, or your bleeding mouth, but I won't stop you if you want to see your children."

Dylan wanted to see his children badly, and even considered the possibility of grabbing a weapon, knife, anything, to fight off the intruders, but thought twice. How would his children react to his physical appearance?

"Daddy! " Angelica called, sounded like she was nearing the bedroom. "I have a headache. Can I sleep with you tonight? I had a nightmare!"

"No, baby," Stella's voice followed. "Let me get you back in bed."

"I want my Daddy!"

Before Dylan had a chance to process everything, his little girl entered the room. Luckily, he'd had a chance to wear the night gown and cover his ruined crotch area.

"Daddy, who are these people? Why is there blood on your mouth?"

Quickly, Jay used a shirt to cover the shotgun that was now on the dresser. "Your daddy had an accident. I'm a doctor, and that nice lady out there is my nurse. We're helping your Daddy."

Angelica must have thought nothing of it, because she sat on the bed.

Dylan ruffled the covers, trying his best to cover any more sign of blood to not scare his daughter.

"What happened Daddy? How did you hurt yourself?"

"I, er, uhm, fell down the stairs."

"You busted your face and your finger fell off?"

It may have sounded absurd, but Dylan knew he had no choice but to feed the bizarre lie to his young daughter. "Yeah, My finger got stuck on something, a nail, and as I fell it pulled off."

"What if I fall down the stairs? Will that happen to me?"

"No, baby. Daddy will fix the stairs so that you are safe."

"Daddy!" Brandon called out, his voice also getting closer. "Mommy is acting weird and says I can't sleep down here tonight."

The boy, being a couple of years older, saw the large man in the bedroom. "Who is this? Is he with Mommy's friend? Why are you hurt, Daddy?"

"Mommy didn't want to tell you, but I fell down the stairs and hurt myself. This man is a doctor, and that nice lady out there is a nurse." Twisted versions of the truth seem to come too easy to him when it came to the safety of his children.

Stella and Elle were both in the doorway and heard the lies. While the children weren't looking, Elle raised the handgun, making Dylan fully aware that she was still in charge.

The gun made Dylan nervous, but was relieved his children were unharmed and that a third intruder hadn't followed them.

"A doctor? He doesn't look like my doctor," Brandon. "My head hurts so bad. Can he help me, too?"

Family Bonding

"I'm not that kind of doctor, little man," Jay said, relaxing his stance. Out of the corner of his eye he saw Elle flashing her weapon to make Dylan nervous, so he shook his head, hoping she'd get the hint to stop. "Uh, maybe you Mommy has some children medicine for headaches?"

"I do," Stella said, noticing that both of her children were still tired, their eyes only half open, and their necks limp. "Maybe I can take you upstairs and tuck you in, while Daddy lets the doctor help him? What do you think, Elle?"

"Well, I suppose all medicine needs a nurse, so sure, I'll tag along."

"Can I have just a second with them, please?" Dylan asked, being sure to use his manners. His arms reached around the children on both sides of him, ignoring the pain from his hand. "If I wasn't hurt, I'd go upstairs and tuck you in, but Daddy needs his own medicine. I just want you two to know how much I love you. I love both of you more than you'll ever realize. Never forget that, no matter what."

"C'mon kiddos. Mommy will fix you right up."

"Daddy, I wish it were you," Angelica said as she leaned in and gave her Daddy a peck on his cheek, trying to avoid any blood smears.

Brandon followed suit, but rather hugged Dylan, awkwardly, trying not to harm his father further. The small arms barely grasped onto Dylan's body.

As they left the room, tears started to fall down Dylan's cheeks. He felt no shame showing his mushy side to Jay, the only one left in the room with him. "I love them so much. Will Elle hurt them? Can I go up there, too?"

"You're not in too much of a shape to venture up a set of stairs," Jay said as he crossed his arms. "Elle won't hurt them, but I'm not sure… Nix that. Nothing."

"No, it's something. What?"

"I pegged you for a goner. All the blood loss, all the pain, yet your kids came, and all of a sudden you got yourself together."

"I don't see the need to scare them any worse than they already are. Is there a third person up there with them?"

Jay raised his eyebrows, unsure how to answer. "Well, at this point, I don't think you're in much shape to fight back or escape or anything. Nope. Nobody up there, well 'cept Elle and Stella right now. Nobody else. We did give them something to help them sleep."

"You really drugged my kids, what if-"

"There's no what if. We had help from a professional."

"You mean to tell me that there's someone out there who's job is to tell you how much drug to give to small children."

"Kinda. Sorta. It's complicated."

"Why are you doing this?"

"Can't really answer that. We've only done this a few times before, and I assure you, children were never harmed in the process."

"Yeah, now I feel so much better."

"Let me ask you, man-to-man. Forget Elle's stupid experiment. Do you still love your wife?"

"Because I had sex with other women? You're a man. You of all people should understand where I'm coming from."

"No, not that. Because your wife has tortured you. You haven't retaliated. You haven't fought back. What gives."

Dylan released an audible sigh and looked Jay in the eyes. "By my math, you and Elle wanted a show. It began with losing a finger, and things escalated from there. I'd much rather be on the receiving end of the pain than the other end. I could never hurt Stell like this. Never. I love her too much."

"What if I make you? What if I think she deserves it?"

"No, not happening."

"Gun to your head change your mind?"

Dylan's voice was quivering. "Nope."

"Gun to your sweet daughter's head change your mind? What if I tell you to hurt your wife, or I'll go upstairs and rape your precious little girl?"

"You're a monster."

"You don't know the full story."

"Then tell me, please."

Jay cleared his throat, and then heard the stairs squeaking. "They're on their way back. Just remember what I've told you."

Reversal

"Are the kids okay, Stell?" Dylan asked. "Jay says they've been drugged."

"They're fine."

Her terse response wounded Dylan emotionally. "How do you know?"

"I know."

"Elle, I've been talking to Dylan here, and guess what?" Jay said, standing taller to exert authority. "He's saying that it would hurt him more to inflict pain on his wife than it would for him to the one hurt."

"And."

"I think it'd be fun to change it up a little bit. What d'ya say?"

"Nu huh," Stella said, standing up. "I'll tell you right now, I'm not sure if I love him after he confirmed that he'd cheated on me. No way would I love him after him physically injuring me."

"Fair is fair, tho, isn't it? Look what you've done to this man, and you're not willing to take any of the pain? Elle, what are your thoughts? This is your experiment."

Elle eyed Jay up and down. "What is this, some bro code or something? You know we're not here for that!"

"Right!" Stella chimed in.

"Dylan," Jay said sympathetically, "bro, you say you won't hurt Stella, right? So you hurting Stella would hurt you? That's what we've been doing. Hurting Dylan."

"Hurting my wife would be worse than any physical pain I've suffered."

"There ya have it!" Jay said with excitement. "See, Elle?"

"I suppose," Elle replied as she raised the handgun towards a nervous Stella with shifty eyes. "I get that logic. You want to hurt your husband? Making him hurt you would wound him deeply, deeper than the sad physical state he's in."

"Yeah, well, I'm not sure if I'm getting better or worse. My balls and all are numb, and at least I can't feel those anymore."

"Oh," Jay gruffed. "That's the hair tie. The sex organ tourniquet. Cutting off the blood flow might have saved your life, but it won't save your beans and frank. We need to get this happening. That sort of thing is time sensitive."

89

"Dylan, would you pull a fingernail from your wife's hand?" Elle asked.

"No."

"That's minor," she said now approaching him with the handgun. "So I'll give you something else. Any thoughts Jay?"

"I've always heard an eye for an eye. A paper cut on her eyeball? I'll hold her down, and keep it open for her. I might even enjoy doing that!"

"Jay! What are you saying?"

"Calm down, Elle. It's a minor injury. I only want to see how she responds. You know, for your," he used his fingers to form air quotes, "experiment."

There was no waiting for Jay to act. With one large hand, he grabbed Stella by her hair, and forced her flat on the bed.

Stella's arms flailed, but Jay gave her a warning that her fighting back wasn't a smart on her part. "I'll gut you like the pig you are!"

This was the first time of the night that Dylan saw a flash of fear in his wife's eyes. "Babe, it's a minor thing. I hate doing it to you, but if it'll save our lives…"

"You're not the one being threatened with your eye being sliced open!" Stella called out. "Please don't!"

"You might be right, Jay," Elle agreed. "She might deserve this. Maybe she really doesn't love him. Probably never did. And it appears he loves her so much. It's stupid, the way she's comparing a small eye slice to him losing a finger, some teeth. His sex parts are in tatters. Let's not forget, she raped him with a lightbulb. Maybe she's too selfish!"

"I've never seen you so passionate about something," Elle rubbed Jay's back, and pointed the weapon directly in Stella's face. "Okay. If you're sure, hold her down. Keep her eye open. I think I'll cross over to your side, Jay. Dylan, instead of a paper cut, grab those tiny scissors she used on your finger. I want to see if eyeballs bleed!"

Dylan could have kicked himself for being so stupid and not realizing that the surgical scissors were on the floor, slightly beneath the bed, but not in plain sight, from where Stella must have dropped them after removing his finger.

After weighing the pros and cons, he now held his own weapon, Dylan realized the short blades were inferior to their bullets. Briefly, it crossed his mind that it might feel good to hurt his wife after everything she had done to him tonight. Half of the pain she inflicted on him wasn't even forced on her by the intruders.

He shook his head, to make the bad thoughts go away. Dylan opened his mouth, but his jaw moved without forming words. After a few seconds of silence, he remembered his role of the night, the game forced upon him, the character he had been playing that caused the home invaders to feel pity, maybe even sympathy for him.

"I love my wife. Too much. I can't hurt her."

Stella smiled so big that she showed her teeth. "See, he's spineless, too. How could I love him?"

Her words sliced his ego in two, so he grasped onto the small scissors tightly.

"Bro," Jay said, "I'll hold her down. Elle keep the gun on her, she might get squirmy again."

"Nope, you can't do this to me! We agreed that-"

Jay used the back of his hand to smack Stella across her face. "Shut up and take a dose of your own medicine. Dylan has earned this. Do it, Dylan! Do it!"

Watching Stella trying to feebly remove Jay's hands from her head was entertaining to watch. Her feminine arms grabbing at his muscular arms only annoyed the large man as he swatted her hands away.

"Elle, put that gun right in her face. Remind her who is in charge here!"

The female intruder did as instructed, but took it a step further.

Stella was mid-scream, her mouth open.

Elle rammed the pistol straight into the open mouth, the metal snagging on teeth, three of them chipping instantly.

This calmed Stella, or at least stopped her from trying to fight.

The sound of Stella breathing through her nose was heavy, and a bubble of snot burst.

Good for the Gander

With Jay now having a free hand, it was much easier for him to place one large finger above Stella's eye, and another below it. Holding it open made it impossible to blink, nevertheless for her to close it completely. "She's ready, Dylan."

Playing into what he thought was an experiment, a game, one that he was winning, Dylan simply said, "No."

"If you don't," Elle warned, "I'll blow her head off right now!"

Realizing there was no use in fighting it, Dylan leaned in towards his wife's head. Once upon a time, he remembered seeing a light of love and kindness in her eyes.

Now, Dylan saw nothing but hatred toppled with fear.

It was like reliving every tortuous act Dylan had experienced for the past few hours, as every single one of his movements stung with nerve endings of fire, his injuries crying out for attention.

Not being able to blink caused her eye to dry out, no longer with a top layer of liquid available to try and protect the sight orb from the soon-to-happen-pain.

Still putting on the show he thought his intruders wanted, Dylan opened the blades of the surgical tool and neared it to his wife's eye. "I really don't think that I can!"

"You can and you will!" Jay encouraged him. "It wouldn't be easy cleaning up Stella's brain matter from this bed!"

The ring-fingerless left hand was no good for Dylan, so he held the scissors with only his right hand, which was shaking. It felt surreal, like it was a cartoon arm stretched out before him, nearing his wife's dry eye.

Jay was doing his job perfectly, holding Stella's head still, but it was Dylan that couldn't control his trembling hand.

The sharp point of the scissors plunged into the spongy substance, and Dylan felt a 'give', like the outer layer (fibrous tunic) gave in to his will of penetration. His intention was a small slash, a straight slash, but it was out of his control.

The opened blade, the sharp side assaulting the vulnerable eye, went jagged, not only scratching more than intended, but also puncturing a hole.

The liquid, white and milky, seeped from the tiny incision.

Stella was wailing like a banshee and Jay was laughing in her face, his spittle coating her forehead.

Dylan knew he had accomplished the task set out for him, but this felt better than he expected. Every ache, especially from his crotch and backside, reminded him that it had been his wife that had cursed his body with pure agony.

A strong urge beckoned to Dylan, begged him to continue elongating the slit.

Before he knew it, he had dragged the scissor blade across her eye, from one side to the next, pressing harder as he went.

If only Stella hadn't been screaming, Dylan could have heard the squashy sounds of fluids leaking. The visual was enough sensation for him to imagine. A milky substance puddled above Stella's lower eyelid, from there it slowly leaked down the side of her head, crossing her temple where it caught in the hairline and disappeared.

Jay and Elle were speaking, Stella was screaming, but Dylan heard nothingness.

Dylan was alone in his head.

Upon reaching the crevice where the eyelids met, he continued to slice, separating the upper and lower eyelids, and followed the white line of liquid goo.

The small portion of thin face flesh parted, creating a larger hole in the area that housed his wife's eyeball. Due to the opening, the side of her eye bulged slightly out of her head, creating a minor droop.

The breaking of skin mixed blood with the white fluid line, combined into the most glorious pink Dylan had ever seen.

It was when he reached her hairline that he realized he had gone too far.

Lifting the scissors from her face snapped Dylan back into reality.

The change was sudden and Dylan's ears tried to take in all the chaos, but his mind was in no shape to comprehend.

Jay lifted his hands from Stella's head. She sat up, her clear tears washing away the pink, some of them catching in the rift of divided skin, salt slightly stinging her gash.

"I'm so sorry," Dylan shed tears also, more than his wife, a sign of his genuine sincerity. "I'm so sorry. I hate myself for doing that! Why did I do that?"

Good for the Goose

Stella was stunned.

Slowly, she looked around the room, surveying the reactions of the other people in the room. Jay was laughing, Elle's mouth hung open, and her husband was sobbing.

In the quest of continuing her experiment, Elle started with her questions. "Dylan, how do you feel? Stella, do you still love your husband?"

"I hate myself, Stell, I'm so sorry," Dylan's voice quivered.

"Good," Stella said with an attitude. "I hate you, too."

"Stell, please don't say that. Please forgive me! I'm begging."

Dylan leaned in close to wrap an arm around his wife to try and console her. For a fleeting moment she seemed welcoming...

Until she took advantage of her husband's guilt and grabbed the small scissors from his hand.

Everything happened so fast and there was no time for Dylan to react.

Stella held the scissors like a knife, gripped tightly in the palm of her hand, the sharp blades sticking out from her smallest finger. She raised the weapon above her head and brought it down with force into the side of Dylan's cheek.

The sharpness punctured a hole, the blades now inside Dylan's mouth, scraping a tooth. Excruciating pain radiated towards his ear, burrowing into the depth of his fragile brain.

With the blades still inside his cheek, Stella pulled towards herself, jerking haphazardly, until flesh separated. The lower side of Dylan's cheek fell loosely to his lower jawline, revealing bloody teeth.

BOOM!

Dylan's ears rang with a high-pitched hissing.

Part Four: When It's All Done and Done

Finality

There was so much mess.

Slime. Blood. Fractured bone.

Dylan was covered in the goop, and it took several moments for him to process what had happened.

Like a baby looking at his own hands for the first time, Dylan spread his fingers, gunk making the webbing of his fingers sticky. The side of his head was covered in the same substance, Stella's brain matter. It was fruitless trying to wipe it from his face. The mess seemed to be gummed onto his skin.

Once Dylan's eyes landed on Stella, her limp body now downed on the bed, it was shocking to see that she no longer had a head. Her neck stump squirted blood like a fountain, festive and red.

"I had to do it, bro," Jay said softly. "She deserved it. More than you'll ever know."

"You may be right," Elle agreed. "Okay, I guess we can leave now."

Ignoring his unwelcomed guests, Dylan cradled his wife's corpse, his arms stiff beneath her. "Baby! No, Stell! No! No! No! No!" His loose jaw skin flapping with each word, his tongue snagging on chipped teeth.

Shaking her body left behind splats of blood on the bed sheets, separate from the puddles.

The intruders collected their items, placing them back inside their black bag of tricks.

"One last thing," Jay said loudly, hoping Dylan would hear him. "I'm leaving your phone in the kitchen. You need to call yourself an ambulance. Sooner than later."

With that, Dylan was alone with his grief.

The Struggle

Dylan's bare feet scrambled their way through the bedroom, stepping on fragments of bone skull. His weak legs gave out, forcing him to crawl through the sludge of body matter.

Getting to his phone was his top priority.

He knew he had lost too much blood and his chances of survival were low.

The hallway between bedroom and kitchen had never felt this far before, but being reduced to dragging his ruined body on the carpet made the trek nearly impossible. Feeling the rawness of his crotch scraping against the fibers had to be ignored for now.

Dylan just knew that he had to get to his phone.

"Brandon! Angelica!"

His screams for his children came out as sounds that weren't recognizable as the names he thought his lips had formed.

True to his word, Jay had left the phone on the edge of the island in the kitchen, the same place where he had found it when they initially invaded the home.

Exhaustion, grief, and suffering overtook Dylan, but he had just enough strength to reach upward, his hand knocking the phone to the floor.

Dialing seemed like an impossible task, but the thought of his children gave him enough willpower to trudge through the pain.

"Hello, what's your emergency?"

Dylan didn't hear a single word.

And his eyes closed before he had a chance to respond.

News Reports

Excerpts from newspapers: digital and print: local and globally.

Dylan Barl, a man tortured by his own wife and intruders, survived multiple surgeries…

…. wife's corpse found with a shotgun wound to the head…

…. a scene that police described as insane and unlike anything they had ever seen before. An insider

reported several officers vomited at the scene, possibly contaminating some of the evidence…

… unnamed Police Officer: "There was so much blood. Dylan was barely alive when we arrived. He was covered in blood, maybe even bone fragments"….

… a bloodied pair of wire pliers found under the bed had the fingerprints of Stella Barl, Eleanor 'Elle' Fime, and Jacob 'Jay' Topps leading the police to the intruders….

… the long awaited trial started yesterday with explosive testimonies….

….a quote from Eleanor Fime: "We're not the masterminds behind this. Stella found us online. Said she was trapped in a loveless marriage with a cheating husband. She hired us to help her torture her husband, she wanted to be the one to hurt him…. We did not hurt Dylan. And we were supposed to kill him, no, she wanted us to make her kill him. To make it look like she had no choice. She wanted to be the one to kill him, then plead her innocence that she was forced to do it….

Stella even stole the drugs from her pharmacy to drug the children so they would sleep through the events. We did not hurt those children. She told me to even kill the dog to make it realistic, like a real home invasion"....

.... A quote from Jacob Topps: "Dylan loved her so much... I couldn't hurt him, but yes, I killed Stella, but she was the one that hired me to kill him. She deserved it. If I hadn't taken the job, someone else would have and killed him. I did not hurt Dylan or the children... Stella wanted to collect his life insurance policy and not have to fight for custody of the children"....

.... We have not yet received a public statement from Dylan Barl...

...

A note from the dark mind of Sea Caummisar

Did anyone see that coming? That Stella was the one who hired Jay and Elle? There are little hints in the story, so I'm not trying to claim that the ending came as a complete shock.

I will say that I am a believer in karma. Maybe Stella did get what she deserved. Maybe she didn't. I judge nobody, not even my fictional characters, but Stella played with fire and got burned.

I suppose, a wife killing her husband for life insurance money and custody of the children is not an original idea... But maybe it's original that Stella set it up so that she could torture her husband and murder him, and plead her innocence by saying that she literally had a gun to her head, making her to commit those vile acts.

What about Dylan's thoughts on cheating? He didn't consider it breaking his wedding vows if it were only physical sex, no emotions attached. Any thoughts on that?

It's fiction, so don't overthink it.

If her plan had worked, maybe Stella could have gotten away with murder, maybe she wouldn't have.

I might know what you're thinking. Stella's plans were a bit drastic. Dylan did love her, but yes he did cheat. Most women wouldn't kill their husbands for having an affair, but I'm willing to bet that some would. Actually, in many true crimes TV shows I watch, many murders are motivated by infidelity.

Is there a lesson to this story?

Probably not.

Maybe there is. Maybe the lesson is that getting away with murder is a hard task. Maybe the lesson is to NOT trust criminals that you meet on the Internet. Maybe the lesson is you shouldn't cheat on your spouse. Maybe the lesson is to never make a woman mad. MAYBE

That's the beauty of fiction. You can read it purely as entertainment, or you can take away something deeper. Did you learn anything from the story? Or did you read it as an escape from real life? I'd love to hear your thoughts.

At the least, I hope you were entertained.

I try to put out at least one novella a month, so be sure to keep up with me for new releases.

If you want to keep up with my releases, I'm on various forms of social media, etc…

If you're like me and don't spend much time on social media, here's a good old fashioned email. sharoncheatham81@gmail.com.

I read often and love Goodreads, too. If you want to keep up with what I'm reading, I'm Sea Caummisar on Goodreads.

Until then, Stay Dark My Friends,
See ya next read,
Your Friend,
Sea Caummisar
Contact Info for Sea Caummisar
Facebook (Sea Caummisar)
Twitter (@seacaummisar)
Goodreads (Sea Caummisar)

Other titles from the dark mind of Sea Caummisar

Standalones

The Absence of Pain: Extreme Horror

Plagued by a rare disease and a lifetime of not being able to feel pain, Huey can't help but be curious as to how pain feels. What better way to explore his unhealthy obsession with pain than to hurt people and ask them how it feels?

Soon, life would take a turn for the worse, and Huey will learn that pain isn't only physical.
Despite the title, this story is full of pain.

Extreme Horror. Graphic scenes of violence.
Includes a bonus short story: PGAD.

The Tata Thief:

Short story: Novelette

Breast cancer and a double mastectomy causes Jill to lose her mind. Unable to afford reconstructive surgery after losing her breasts forces her to find creative ways to replace her bosom.
This is a violent book.

The Punched Line:

A struggling comedian, trying to make a name for himself, gets offered a gig that can make or break his career.

Meanwhile, a murder contract is placed on the dark web to ensure that the show is very eventful.

Warning: Graphic scenes of violence

Short story: Novelette

Frut of Her Loins: Extreme Horror

FRUT: (urban dictionary); frequently recycled used trash: used damaged goods, trash, person/ object/ or action, a rubbish person in behavior and habit.

An online identity, simply know as Frut/of/Her/Loins, makes a living by selling fruit (or other food) that has been inserted into her vagina for one full day. Needless to say, her website business is more profitable than one would imagine.

A grieving housewife finds out that her husband has been a customer of Frut/of/Her/Loins. She gathers a group of angry wives and hunts down the woman behind the acts that they consider vile.

This a very violent book.
You have been warned.
Novella

The Art of Human Hunting: Extreme Horror

Once a year, a group of friends meet to hunt humans.

After the hunt, they each partake in a pain competition where they are each given one minute to hurt their victim.

Finally, they each get a chance to turn their victim into a work of art.

Follow Scott's journey and his first year in 'The Hunt'.

Warning: This is a violent book with scenes of torture

With Child: Extreme Horror

After three pregnant patients go missing after last being seen at Dr. Marsh's OB-GYN office, he becomes a prime suspect in the missing person cases. Dr. Marsh prides himself on being an upstanding citizen. Not only does he donate time and money to several charities, he is also a caring doctor.Is he a nice person? Or is he as evil as the police suspect?EXTREME HORROR: There are multiple scenes of violence, blood, gore, and torture. Most of the torture is against a pregnant woman, being held captive against her will.

Scatology

Scatology: An interest in or preoccupation with excrement and excretion. Coprophilia: Abnormal interest and pleasure in feces and defecation. Meet Luke. This is the tale of his quest to find love and acceptance despite his unique sexual desires. Warning: There are some scenes of the sexual nature. There are some gross scenes and a mild level of violence.

Dr. Circumcision, Quack MD

Circumcision: the removal of the foreskin from the human penis
Female Circumcision: practice of cutting off the clitoris and sometimes the labia

Not all doctors have a license to practice medicine.

This is a story of one particular unlicensed doctor that is obsessed with the surgical procedure of circumcision.

WARNING: Intended for mature audiences. Extreme scenes of violence and gore.

Marsha's Morbid Museum of Macabre

Marsha's fascination with displaying corpses in her home started in an innocent fashion.

Now, bored with her wealth, she has found that she enjoys fusing human bodies and animals together.

When her loyal maid, Sylvia, stumbles upon her secret, how will she react?

Warning: This isn't a very bloody book, however there are a couple scenes that deal with animals. If you have any sort of animal sensitivity.... this might not be the book for you.

Gambler's Appetite of Remorse

Jon's gambling habit is out of control. Not only has he lost all of his money, he also lost his sanity.

His wife is not happy with him since they have no money for food.

Jon finds a new way of life which enables him to find free food. (He gets very creative.)

Every time he 'finds' money, he takes it back to the casino, only to lose it again.

Then he gets resourceful in finding a source of entertainment. Such as kidnapping people and making them gamble for blood.

WARNING this book is for a mature audience. There are graphic scenes of grossness, violence, and gore. (and some comedy)

Til Death Do Us Part

On New Year's Eve, Cole is waiting outside a party for his wife to leave with her current lover.

Cole's resolution is to make sure his wife sticks to her marriage vows. Since he agreed to love her til death do them part, why couldn't she? His only goal is to make those words come true.

The things he wants to do to his wife and her lover are unspeakable.

This is a violent book. There is a ton of blood. If you can't handle a few chapters of descriptive gore, then this book is not for you. Maybe I should add triggers, but instead let's just call it EXTREME HORROR.

An Extreme Turkey Dinner

After a terrible family tragedy, what seems like a peaceful Thanksgiving meal turns into a meal of horror.

Angie has hit the breaking point with her family. That doesn't deter her from wanting to spend a holiday with her family.

The guests soon find out that Angie didn't invite them out of kindness.

This is a bloody horror story. There are scenes of extreme violence. Not for children.

This story is based on fiction. If this is anything like your family holidays, I apologize.

Punpkins for Cheap: A Grotesque Horror (Novelette)

JUST IN TIME FOR HALLOWEEN!

TRICK OR TREAT?

The first story is the trick

The second story is the treat

'PUNPKINS FOR CHEAP'

This book should never be read by anyone. It's gross and immature. It's almost as if a small child wrote it. If you enjoy poorly written dark humor, you might like this book. I mean, there's a chapter titled 'Tampons Are Not Yummy'. So use your imagination as to what kind of story this is.

PLUS A BONUS STORY TITLED 'THEM BONES'

'Them Bones' is the most disturbing story I have ever written. It is true body horror! Probably one of the most twisted and bloodiest stories I have ever written. No spoilers, but it's about a man who falls in love with a skeleton. The skeleton asks him to make her pretty.

PROCEED WITH CAUTION MATURE AUDIENCES ONLY

TWO EXTREME SHORT STORIES

The Psycho Logic Of Al: Extreme Horror

After a life of hardships, Al travels the world doing what he enjoys most. Murdering people and wishing for death, but having fun in the process. Then he meets Sally and his entire world changes.

Fictional psychos can be logical.

Or crazy.

Whichever is more entertaining.

Warning: Extreme horror, graphic scenes that may disturb some readers

Completed Series
Deadly Reality TV Books 1-4 (would you hurt yourself for money?)
Verdict Realty Books 1-3   (a serial killer realtor)
Damon Dahmer and Sly Verdict Books 1-2
Games Series Books 1-6   (a game with a deadly twist)
Sanger Entertainment Books 1-5 (spinoff of Games series)

Incomplete Series
My Fan (1-2-3)
Acrotomophilia Maniac (1-2)
Raised by a Killer (1, 2, 3,4,5, 6, 7)

See ya next read

Printed in Great Britain
by Amazon